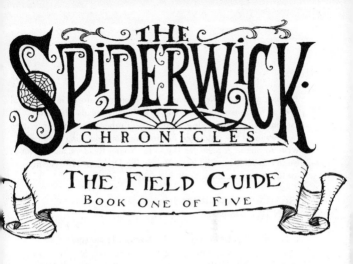

THE SPIDERWICK CHRONICLES

THE FIELD GUIDE

BOOK ONE OF FIVE

Tony DiTerlizzi *and* Holly Black

SCHOLASTIC INC.

New York Toronto London Auckland Sydney
Mexico City New Delhi Hong Kong Buenos Aires

ISBN-13: 978-0-545-07170-3
ISBN-10: 0-545-07170-4

Copyright © 2003 by Tony DiTerlizzi and Holly Black.
All rights reserved. Published by Scholastic Inc., 557 Broadway, New York, NY 10012, by arrangement with Simon & Schuster Books for Young Readers, an imprint of Simon & Schuster Children's Publishing Division. SCHOLASTIC and associated logos are trademarks and/or registered trademarks of Scholastic Inc.

12 11 10 9 8 7 6 5 4 3 2 1   8 9 10 11 12 13/0

Printed in the U.S.A.   23

This edition first printing, February 2008

Book design by Tony DiTerlizzi and Dan Potash

For my grandmother, Melvina,
who said I should write a book just like this one
and to whom I replied that I never would
—H. B.

For Arthur Rackham,
may you continue to inspire others
as you have me
—T. D.

Table of Contents

List of Full-Page Illustrations

Dear Reader,

Over the years that Tony and I have been
friends, we've shared the same childhood
fascination with faeries. We did not realize
the importance of that bond or how it might be
tested.

One day Tony and I—along with several other
authors—were doing a signing at a large bookstore.
When the signing was over, we lingered, helping
to stack books and chatting, until a clerk
approached us. He said that there had been a
letter left for us. When I inquired which one
us, we were surprised by his answer.

"Both of you," he said.

The letter was exactly as reproduced on the
following page. Tony spent a long time just
staring at the photocopy that came with it.
Then, in a hushed voice, he wondered aloud about
the remainder of the manuscript. We hurriedly
wrote a note, tucked it back into the envelope
and asked the clerk to deliver it to the Grace
children.

Not long after, a package arrived on my
doorstep, bound in red ribbon. A few days after
that, three children rang the bell and told me
this story.

What has happened since is hard to describe.
Tony and I have been plunged into a world we
never quite believed in. We now see that faeries
are far more than childhood stories. There is a
invisible world around us and we hope that you,
dear reader, will open your eyes to it.

HOLLY BLACK

Dear Mrs. Black and Mr. DiTerlizzi:

I know that a lot of people don't believe in faeries, but I do and I think that you do too. After I read your books, I told my brothers about you and we decided to write. We know about real faeries. In fact, we know a lot about them.

The page attached to this one is a photocopy from an old book we found in our attic. It isn't a great copy because we had some trouble with the copier. The book tells people how to identify faeries and how to protect themselves. Can you please give this book to your publisher? If you can, please put a letter in this envelope and give it back to the store. We will find a way to send the book. The normal mail is too dangerous.

We just want people to know about this. The stuff that has happened to us could happen to anyone.

Sincerely,

Mallory, Jared, and Simon Grace

It was more like a dozen shacks.

Chapter One

IN WHICH the Grace Children Get Acquainted with Their New Home

If someone had asked Jared Grace what jobs his brother and sister would have when they grew up, he would have had no trouble replying. He would have said that his brother, Simon, would be either a veterinarian or a lion tamer. He would have said that his sister, Mallory, would either be an Olympic fencer or in jail for stabbing someone with a sword. But he couldn't say what job he would grow up to have. Not that anyone asked him. Not that anyone asked his opinion on anything at all.

1

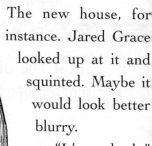

JARED GRACE

The new house, for instance. Jared Grace looked up at it and squinted. Maybe it would look better blurry.

"It's a shack," Mallory said, getting out of the station wagon.

It wasn't really, though. It was more like a dozen shacks had been piled on top of one another. There were several chimneys, and the whole thing was topped off by a strip of iron fence sitting on the roof like a particularly garish hat.

"It's not so bad," their mother said, with a smile

2

that looked only slightly forced. "It's Victorian."

Simon, Jared's identical twin, didn't look upset. He was probably thinking of all the animals he could have now. Actually, considering what he'd packed into their tiny bedroom in New York, Jared figured it would take a lot of rabbits and hedgehogs and whatever else was out here to satisfy Simon.

SIMON GRACE

"Come on, Jared," Simon called. Jared realized that they had all crossed to the front steps and he was alone on the lawn, staring at the house.

3

The doors were a faded gray, worn with age. The only traces of paint were an indeterminate cream, stuck deep in crevices and around the hinges. A rusted ram's-head door knocker hung from a single, heavy nail at its center.

Their mother fit a jagged key into the lock, turned it, and shoved hard with her shoulder.

The door opened into a dim hallway. The only window was halfway up the stairs, and its stained glass panes gave the walls an eerie, reddish glow.

"It's just like I remember," she said, smiling.

"Only crappier," said Mallory.

Their mother sighed but didn't otherwise respond.

The hallway led into a dining room. A long table with faded water spots was the only piece of furniture. The plaster ceiling was cracked in places and a chandelier hung from frayed wires.

"Why don't you three start bringing things in from the car?" their mother said.

"Into here?" Jared asked.

"Yes, into here." Their mother put down her suitcase on the table, ignoring the eruption of dust. "If your great-aunt Lucinda hadn't let us stay, I don't know where we would have gone. We should be grateful."

None of them said anything. Try as he might, Jared didn't feel anything close to grateful. Ever since their dad moved out everything had gone bad. He'd messed up a school, and the fading bruise over his left eye wouldn't let him forget it. But this place—this place was the worst yet.

"Jared," his mother said as he turned to follow Simon out to unload the car.

"What?"

His mother waited until the other two were down the hall before she spoke. "This is a chance to start over . . . for all of us. Okay?"

Jared nodded grudgingly. He didn't need her to say the rest of it—that the only reason he hadn't gotten kicked out of school was because they were moving anyway. Another reason he was supposed to be grateful. Only he wasn't.

Outside, Mallory had stacked two suitcases on top of a steamer trunk. "I heard she's starving herself to death."

"Aunt Lucinda? She's just old," said Simon. "Old and crazy."

But Mallory shook her head. "I heard Mom on the phone. She was telling Uncle Terrence that Aunt Lucy thinks little men bring her food."

"What do you expect? She's in a nuthouse," Jared said.

Mallory went on like she hadn't heard him. "She told the doctors the food she got was better than anything they'd ever taste."

"You're making that up." Simon crawled into the backseat and opened one of the suitcases.

7

Mallory shrugged. "If she dies, this place is going to get inherited by someone, and we're going to have to move again."

"Maybe we can go back to the city," Jared said.

"Fat chance," said Simon. He took out a wad of tube socks. "Oh, no! Jeffrey and Lemondrop chewed their way loose!"

"Mom told you not to bring the mice," Mallory said. "She said you could have *normal* animals now."

"If I let them go, they'd get stuck in a glue trap or something," said Simon, turning a sock inside out, one finger sticking out a hole. "Besides, you brought all your fencing junk!"

"It's not junk," Mallory growled. "And it's not *alive*."

"Shut up!" Jared took a step toward his sister.

"Just because you've got one black eye

doesn't mean I can't give you another one." Mallory flipped her ponytail as she turned toward him. She shoved a heavy suitcase into his hands. "Go ahead and carry that if you're so tough."

Even though Jared knew he might be bigger and stronger than her someday—when she wasn't thirteen and he wasn't nine—it was hard to picture.

Jared managed to lug the suitcase inside the door before he dropped it. He figured he could drag it the rest of the way if he had to and no one would be the wiser. Alone in the hallway of the house, however, Jared no longer remembered how to get to the dining room. Two different hallways split off this one, winding deep into the middle of the house.

"Mom?" Although he'd meant to call out loudly, his voice sounded very soft, even to himself.

"Mom?"

No answer. He took a tentative step and then another, until the creak of a board under his feet stopped him.

Just as he paused, something *inside* the wall rustled. He could hear it scrabbling upward, until the sound disappeared past the ceiling. His heart beat hard against his chest.

It's probably just a squirrel, he told himself. After all, the house looked like it was falling apart. Anything could be living inside; they'd be lucky if there wasn't a bear in the basement and birds in all the heating ducts. That was, if the place even *had* heat.

"Mom?" he said again, even more faintly.

Then the door behind him opened and Simon came in, carrying mason jars with two bug-eyed gray mice in them. Mallory was right behind him, scowling.

"I heard something," Jared said. "In the wall."

"What?" Simon asked.

"I don't know. . . ." Jared didn't want to admit that for a moment he'd thought it was a ghost. "Probably a squirrel."

Simon looked at the wall with interest. Brocaded gold wallpaper hung limply, peeling and pocking in places. "You think so? In the house? I always wanted a squirrel."

No one seemed to think that something in the walls was anything to worry about, so Jared didn't say anything more about it. But as he carried the suitcase to the dining room, Jared couldn't help thinking about their tiny apartment in New York and their family before the divorce. He wished this was some kind of gimmicky vacation and not real life.

The creak startled him into jerking upright.

Chapter Two

IN WHICH Two Walls Are Explored by Vastly Different Methods

The leaks in the roof had made all but three of the upstairs bedroom floors danger-usly rotted. Their mother got one, Mallory got nother, and Jared and Simon were left to share ne third.

By the time they were done unpacking, the ressers and nightstands of Simon's side of the oom were covered in glass tanks. A few were lled with fish. The rest were crammed with ice, lizards, and other animals that Simon had onfined to mud-furnished cages. Their mother

MALLORY GRACE

had told Simon h
could bring every
thing but the mice
She thought the
were disgustin,
because Simo
had rescue
them from
trap in Mrs
Levette's down
stairs apartment
She pretended no
to notice he'd brough
them anyway.

Jared tossed and turned o
the lumpy mattress, pressing the pillow dow
over his head like he was smothering himself, bu
he couldn't sleep. He didn't mind sharing a room
with Simon, but sharing a room with cages o

nimals that rustled, squeaked, and scratched
vas eerier than sleeping alone would have been.
t made him think of the thing in the walls. He'd
hared a room with Simon and the critters in the
ity, but the animal noises had dimmed against
he background of cars and sirens and people.
Iere, everything was unfamiliar.

The creak of hinges startled him into jerk-
ng upright. There was a figure in the doorway,
vith a shapeless white gown and long, dark
air. Jared slid off the bed so fast he didn't
ven remember doing it.

"It's just me," the figure whispered. It was
Mallory in a nightgown. "I think I heard your
quirrel."

Jared stood up from a crouch, trying to
lecide if moving so fast meant he was a chicken
r if he just had good reflexes. Simon was snor-
ng gently in the other bed.

Mallory put her hands on her hips. "Come on. It's not going to wait around for us to catch it."

Jared shook his twin's shoulder. "Simon. Wake up. New pet. New peeeeeeeeeet."

Simon twitched and groaned, trying to pull the covers over his head.

Mallory laughed.

"Simon." Jared leaned in close, making his voice deliberately urgent. "Squirrel! Squirrel!"

Simon opened his eyes and glared at them. "I was sleeping."

"Mom went out to the store for milk and cereal," Mallory said, pulling the covers off him. "She said I was supposed to keep an eye on you. We don't have much time before she gets back."

The three siblings crept along the dark hallways of their new house. Mallory was in the lead, walking a few paces and then stopping to listen. Every now and then there would be a scratch or a sound like small footsteps inside the walls.

The scuttling grew louder as they neared the kitchen. In the kitchen sink, Jared could see a pan crusted with the remains of the macaroni and cheese they'd had for dinner.

"I think it's there. Listen," Mallory whispered.

The sound stopped completely.

Mallory picked up a broom and held the wooden end like a baseball bat. "I'm going to knock open the wall," she said.

"Mom is going to see the hole when she gets back," Jared said.

"In this house? She'll never notice."

"What if you hit the squirrel?" Simon asked. "You could hurt—"

"Shhhh," Mallory said. She padded across the floor in her bare feet and swung the broom handle at the wall. The blow broke through the plaster, scattering dust like flour. It settled in Mallory's hair, making her look even more ghostly. She reached into the hole and broke off a chunk of the wall.

Jared stepped closer. He could feel the hair on his arms stand up.

Torn strips of cloth had been wadded up between the boards. As she snapped off more pieces, other things were revealed. The remains of curtains. Bits of tattered silk and lace. Straight pins poked into the wooden beams on either side, making a strange upward-snaking line. A doll's head lolled in one corner. Dead cockroaches were strung up like garlands. Tiny lead soldiers with melted hands and feet were scattered across the planks like a fallen army

"I'm going to knock open the wall."

Jagged pieces of mirror glittered from where they had been glued with ancient gum.

Mallory reached into the nest and took out a fencing medal. It was silver with a thick blue ribbon. "This is mine."

"The squirrel must have stolen it," said Simon.

"No—this is too weird," Jared said.

"Dianna Beckley had ferrets, and they used to steal her Barbie dolls," Simon replied. "And lots of animals like shiny things."

"But look." Jared pointed to the cockroaches. "What ferret makes his own gross knickknacks?"

"Let's pull this stuff out of here," Mallory

said. "Maybe if it doesn't have a nest, it will be easier to keep out of the house."

Jared hesitated. He didn't want to put his hands inside the wall and feel around. What if it was still in there and bit him? Maybe he didn't know much, but he really didn't think squirrels were normally this creepy. "I don't think we should do that," he said.

Mallory wasn't listening. She was busy dragging over a trash can. Simon started pulling out wads of the musty cloth.

"There's no droppings, either. That's strange." Simon dumped what he was holding and pulled out another handful. At the army men, he stopped. "These are cool, aren't they, Jared?"

Jared had to nod. "They'd be better with hands, though."

Simon put several in the pocket of his pajamas.

"Simon?" Jared asked. "Have you ever heard of an animal like this? I mean, some of this stuff is really odd, you know? Like this squirrel must be as demented as Aunt Lucy."

"Yeah, it's real nutty," Simon said, and giggled.

Mallory groaned, then suddenly went quiet. "I hear it again."

"What?" Jared asked.

"The noise. Shhhh. It's over there." Mallory picked up the broom again.

"Quiet," Simon whispered.

"We're being quiet," Mallory hissed back.

"Shush," Jared said.

The three of them crept over to where the sound came from, just as the noise itself changed. Instead of hearing the clatter of little claws scrabbling on wood, they could clearly hear the scrape of nails on metal.

"Look." Simon bent down to touch a small sliding door set into the wall.

"It's a dumbwaiter," Mallory said. "Servants used it to send trays of breakfast and stuff upstairs. There must be another door like this in one of the bedrooms."

"That thing sounds like it's in the shaft," Jared said.

Mallory leaned her whole body into the metal box. "It's too small for me. One of you is going to have to go."

Simon looked at her skeptically. "I don't know. What if the ropes aren't that good anymore?"

"It would just be a short fall," Mallory said, and both the boys looked at her in astonishment.

"Oh, fine, I'll go." Jared was pleased to find something Mallory couldn't do. She looked a little bit put out. Simon just looked worried.

The inside was dirty and it smelled like old wood. Jared folded his legs in and bent his head forward. He fit, but only barely.

"Is the squirrel-thing even still in the dumbwaiter shaft?" Simon's voice sounded tinny and distant.

"I don't know," Jared said softly, listening to the echoes of his words. "I don't hear anything."

Mallory pulled the rope. With a little jolt and some shaking, the dumbwaiter began to move Jared up inside the wall. "Can you see anything?"

"No," Jared called. He could hear the

scratching sound, but it was distant. "It's completely black."

Mallory winched the dumbwaiter back down. "There's got to be a light around here somewhere." She opened a few drawers until she found the stub of a white candle and a mason jar. Turning a knob on the stove, she lit the wick off one of the gas burners, dripped hot wax into the jar, and pressed the candle against it to hold it in place. "Here, Jared. Hold this."

"Mallory, I don't even hear the thing anymore," said Simon.

"Maybe it's hiding," said Mallory, and yanked on the rope.

Jared tried to tuck himself deeper into the dumbwaiter, but there was no room. He wanted to tell them that this was stupid and that he'd chickened out, but he said nothing. Instead, he let himself be raised into the darkness, holding the makeshift lantern.

The metal box went up a few feet inside the wall. The light from the candle was a small halo, reflecting things erratically. The squirrel-thing could have been right next to him, almost touching him, and he would not have noticed it.

"I don't see anything," he called down, but he wasn't sure if anyone heard him.

The ascent was slow. Jared felt like he couldn't breathe. His knees were pressing against his chest, and his feet were cramping from being bent so long. He wondered if the candle was sucking up all the available oxygen.

Then, with a jerk, the dumbwaiter stopped. Something scraped against the metal box.

"It won't go any farther," Mallory called up the chute. "Do you see anything?"

The dumbwaiter began to move.

Jared wasn't sure where he was.

"No," said Jared. "I think it's stuck."

There was more scraping now, as though something was trying to claw through the top of the dumbwaiter. Jared yelped and tried to pound from the inside, hoping to frighten it off.

Just as suddenly, the dumbwaiter slid up an extra few feet and came to a halt again, this time in a room dimly lit by moonlight from a single, small window.

Jared scrambled out of the box. "I made it! I'm upstairs."

The room had a low ceiling, and the walls were covered in bookshelves. Looking around, he realized there was no door.

All of a sudden, Jared wasn't sure where he was.

Jared looked around the room.

Chapter Three

IN WHICH There Are Many Riddles

Jared looked around the room. It was a smallish library, with one huge desk in the center. On it was an open book and a pair of old-fashioned, round glasses that caught the candlelight. Jared walked closer. The dim glow illuminated one title at a time as he scanned the shelves. They were all strange: *A Historie of Scottish Dwarves, A Compendium of Brownie Visitations from Around the World,* and *Anatomy of Insects and Other Flying Creatures.*

A collection of glass jars containing berries,

dried plants, and one filled with dull river stones sat at the edge of the desk. Nearby, a watercolor sketch showed a little girl and a man playing on the lawn. Jared's eyes fell on a note tossed on top of an open book, both coated in a thin layer of dust. The paper was yellowed with age, but handwritten on it was a strange little poem:

> *In a man's torso you will find*
> *My secret to all mankind*
> *If false and true can be the same*
> *You will soon know of my fame*
> *Up and up and up again*
> *Good luck dear friend*

He picked it up and read it through carefully. It was as though a message had been left here just for him. But by whom? What did the poem mean?

He heard a shout from downstairs. "Mallory! Simon! What are you doing up?"

Jared groaned. It just figured that Mom would get back from the store *now*.

"There was a squirrel in the wall," Jared could hear Mallory say.

Their mother cut her off. "Where's Jared?"

Neither of his siblings said anything.

"You bring that dumbwaiter down. If your brother is in there . . ."

Jared ran over in time to watch the box disappear down into the wall. His candle choked on wax and sputtered from his sudden movement, but it didn't go out.

"See?" Simon said weakly.

The dumbwaiter must have showed up, empty.

"Well, where is he then?"

"I don't know," Mallory said. "In bed, asleep?"

Their mother sighed. "Well, go on, both of you, and join him. Now!"

Jared listened to their retreating steps. They'd have to wait a while before they snuck back down to get him. That is, if they didn't just figure that the dumbwaiter had taken him all the way upstairs. They'd probably be surprised *ot* to find him in bed. How could they know he vas trapped in a room without a door?

There was a rustling behind him. Jared pun around. It came from the desk.

As he held up the makeshift lamp, Jared saw hat something had been scrawled in the dust of he desk. Something that wasn't there before.

Click clack, watch your back.

Jared jumped, causing his candle to tilt. Running wax snuffed the flame. He stood in he darkness, so scared he could barely move. Something was here, in the room, and it could vrite!

He backed toward the empty chute, biting :he inside of his lip to keep from screaming. He :ould hear the rustling of bags downstairs as his mother unpacked groceries.

"What are you?"

"What's there?" he whispered into the darkness. "What are you?"

Only silence answered him.

"I know you're there," Jared said.

But there was no reply and no more rustling. Then he heard his mother on the stairs, a door, and nothing. Nothing but a silence so thick and heavy that it choked him. He felt that even breathing too loudly would give him away. Any moment the thing would be upon him.

There was a creak from inside the wall. Startled, Jared dropped the jar, then realized it was only the dumbwaiter. He felt his way through the darkness.

"Get in," his sister whispered up the shaft.

Jared squeezed into the metal box. He was so filled with relief that he barely noticed the ride down to the kitchen.

As soon as he got out, he started speaking.

"There was a library! A secret library with weird books. And something was in there—it wrote in the dust."

"*Shhhh*, Jared," Simon said. "Mom's going to hear us."

Jared held up the piece of paper with the poem on it. "Look at this. It has some kind of directions on it."

"Did you actually *see* anything?" Mallory asked.

"I saw the message in the dust. It said 'watch your back,'" Jared replied hotly.

Mallory shook her head. "That could have been written there ages ago."

"It wasn't," Jared insisted. "I saw the desk and there was nothing written there before."

"Calm down," Mallory said.

"Mallory, I saw it!"

Mallory grabbed his shirt in her fist. "Be quiet!"

"Mallory! Let go of your brother!" Their mother was standing at the top of the narrow kitchen stairs wearing a less-than-pleased expression. "I thought we already went through this. If I see any of you out of your beds, I am going to lock you in your rooms."

Mallory let go of Jared's shirt with a long glare.

"What if we need to go to the bathroom?" Simon asked.

"Just go to bed," their mother said.

When they got upstairs, Jared and Simon went off to their room. Jared pulled the covers over his head and scrunched his eyes shut.

"I believe you . . . about the note and all," Simon whispered, but Jared didn't reply. He was just glad to be in bed. He thought he could probably stay there for a whole week.

"Just chop it."

Chapter Four

IN WHICH There Are Answers, Although Not Necessarily to the Right Questions

Jared woke up to the sound of Mallory's screaming. He jumped out of bed and rushed down the hall, past Simon, and into his sister's room. Long pieces of her hair had been knotted to the brass headboard. Her face was red, but the worst part was the strange pattern of bruises that decorated her arms. Their mother was seated on the mattress, her fingers tugging at the knots.

"What happened?" Jared asked.

"Just chop it," Mallory sobbed. "Cut it off.

HELEN GRACE

I want to get out of this bed! I want out of this house! I hate this place!"

"Who did this?" Their mother looked at Jared angrily.

"I don't know!" Jared glanced at Simon, standing in the doorway, looking puzzled. It must have been the thing in the walls.

Their mother's eyes got huge. It was scary. "Jared Grace, I saw you arguing with your sister last night!"

"Mom, I didn't do it. Honest." He was shocked that she thought he would do something like this. He and Mallory were always fighting, but it didn't mean anything.

"Get the scissors, Mom!" Mallory yelled.

"Both of you. Out. Jared, I will talk to you later." Mrs. Grace turned back to her daughter.

Jared left the room, his heart pounding. When he thought about Mallory's knotted hair, he couldn't contain a shiver.

"You think that thing did it, don't you?" Simon asked as they entered the bedroom.

Jared looked at his brother in dismay. "Don't you?"

Simon nodded.

"I keep thinking about that poem I found," Jared said. "It's the only clue we have."

"How is a stupid poem going to help?"

"I don't know." Jared sighed. "You're the

smart one. You should be figuring this out."

"How come nothing happened to us? Or to Mom?"

Jared hadn't even thought about that. "I don't know," he said again.

Simon gave him a long look.

"Well? What do *you* think?" Jared asked.

Simon started out the door. "I don't know what I think. I'm going to go try and catch some crickets."

Jared watched him go and wondered what he could do. Could he really solve anything by himself?

Getting dressed, he thought about the poem. "Up and up and up again" was the simplest line, but what did it mean exactly? Up in the house? Up on the roof? Up in a tree? Maybe the poem was just something that an old, dead relative was keeping around—

omething that wasn't going to help at all.

But since Simon was feeding his animals
nd Mallory was being freed from her bed, he
ad nothing better to do than wonder how far
up and up and up again" he needed to go.

So, okay. Maybe it wasn't the easiest clu[e] after all. But Jared figured it couldn't hurt to g[o] up, past the second floor, to the attic.

The stairs were worn clean of their pain[t] and several times the boards he stepped o[n] creaked so dramatically that Jared was afrai[d] they were going to snap from his weight.

The attic level was a vast room with a slante[d] ceiling and a gaping hole in the floor on one en[d]. Through it, he could see down into one of th[e] unusable bedrooms.

Old garment bags hung from a clothesline [o]thin wire stretching across the width of the atti[c]. Birdhouses hung in profusion from the rafter[s] and a dressmaker's dummy stood alone in a co[r]ner, a hat over its knobbed head. And in the ce[n]ter of the room, there was a spiral staircase.

Up and up and up again. Jared took th[e] stairs two at a time.

Up and up and up again

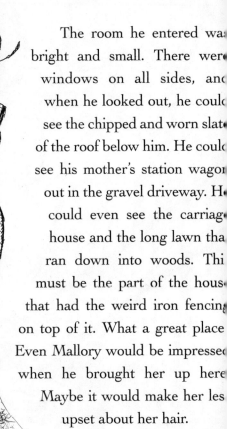

The room he entered was bright and small. There were windows on all sides, and when he looked out, he could see the chipped and worn slate of the roof below him. He could see his mother's station wagon out in the gravel driveway. He could even see the carriage house and the long lawn that ran down into woods. This must be the part of the house that had the weird iron fencing on top of it. What a great place! Even Mallory would be impressed when he brought her up here. Maybe it would make her less upset about her hair.

There wasn't much in

50

In a man's torso
you will find

My secret
to all mankind

If false and true
can be the same

You will soon know
of my fame

Up and up and up
again

Good luck dear friend

Handwritten note uncovered by Jared Grace in Arthur Spiderwick's upstairs library

he room. An old trunk, a small stool, a
Victrola, and rolls of faded fabric.

Jared sat down, pulled the crumpled poem
from his pocket, and read it through again. "In
a man's torso, you will find my secret to all
mankind." Those lines bothered him. He didn't
want to find an old, dead body, even if there
was something really cool inside it.

The bright yellow sunlight splashing across
he floor reassured him. In movies, bad things
seldom happened in broad daylight, but he still
hesitated to open the trunk.

Maybe he should go outside and get Simon
to come up with him. But what if the chest was
empty? Or what if the poem had nothing to do
with Mallory's bruises and knotted hair?

Not knowing what else to do, he knelt down
and brushed cobwebs and grime from the top
of the trunk. Heavy strips of rusted metal

striped the rotting leather. At least he could take a look. Maybe the clue would be more obvious if he knew what was inside.

Taking a breath, Jared pushed up the lid. I was full of very old, moth-eaten clothes Underneath, there was a pocket watch on a long chain, a tattered cap, and a leather satchel full of old, odd-looking pencils and cracked bits of charcoal.

Nothing in the trunk looked like it was a secret, for mankind or anybody else.

Nothing looked like a dead body, either.

"In a man's torso, you will find my secret to all mankind."

He looked down at the contents of the chest again, and it hit him.

He was looking at a *chest*. A man's torso would be his *chest*.

Jared groaned in frustration. How could he

be right and still have nothing to show for it? There was nothing good in the chest, and the other lines of the poem made no sense at all. "If false and true can be the same, you will soon know of my fame." How could that be answered with something real? It sounded like a word game.

What could be false, though? Something about this situation? Something about the stuff

in the chest? The chest itself? He thought about chests, and chests made him think about pirates on a beach, burying treasure deep in the cool sand.

Buried underneath! Not a false chest, but a chest with a false bottom! Looking carefully, he could see that the inside seemed higher than it should be. Had he really solved the riddle?

Jared got down on his knees and began to push all over the floor of the trunk, threading his fingers through the dust to look for seams that might allow him to pull an unseen compartment open. When he found nothing, he began to touch the outside, pawing over the box. Finally, when he pressed three fingers against the edge of the left side, a compartment popped open.

Excited beyond reason, Jared pressed his

hand inside. The only contents were a squar-
ish bundle, wrapped in a dirty cloth. He took
it out, untied it, and started to unfold the fabric from an old, crumbling book that smelled
like burnt paper. Embossed on the brown
leather, the title read: *Arthur Spiderwick's Field
Guide to the Fantastical World Around You.*

The cover was ragged at the edges, and as
he opened it, he noticed that it was full of
watercolor sketches. The writing had been

The strangest thing

done in ink, grown smudged and spotted with age and water damage. He flipped the pages quickly, glancing at notes tucked into the volume. These were written in a spidery hand very like the writing of the riddle.

The strangest thing, however, was the subject matter. The book was full of information about faeries.

He just wanted to keep reading.

Chapter Five

IN WHICH Jared Reads a Book and Sets a Trap

Mallory and Simon were out on the lawn, fencing, when Jared found them. Mallory's ponytail stuck out of the back of her fencing helmet, and Jared could see that it was shorter than it had once been. She was apparently trying to make up for her earlier weakness by ruthless fencing. Simon couldn't seem to get a strike in at all. He was being backed against the side of the broken-down carriage house, his parries becoming increasingly desperate.

"I found something!" Jared called.

Simon turned his helmeted head. Mallory took that opportunity to strike, pushing the rubber tip of her fencing foil against his chest.

"That's three to zip," Mallory said. "I creamed you."

"You cheated," he complained.

"You allowed yourself to become distracted," Mallory countered.

Simon pulled the helmet off his head, flung it down, and looked at Jared.

"Thanks a lot."

"Sorry," Jared said automatically.

"You're the one that always fences with her. I just came out here to catch tadpoles." Simon scowled.

"Well, I was busy. Just because I don't have a bunch of dumb animals to take care of doesn't mean I can't be busy," Jared shot back.

"Just shut up, both of you." Mallory took off her own helmet. Her face was flushed. "What did you find?"

Jared tried to recapture some of his earlier excitement. "A book in the attic. It's about faeries, real faeries. Look, they're ugly."

Mallory took the book out of his hands and looked it over. "This is baby stuff. A storybook."

"It's not," Jared said defensively. "It's a *field guide*. You know, like for birds. So you know how to spot the different kinds."

"You think a *faerie* tied my hair to my bed?"

Mallory asked. "Mom thinks you did. She thinks you've been acting weird ever since Dad left. Like getting into all those fights at school.'"

Simon didn't say anything.

"But *you* don't think that." Jared hoped she would agree. "And you *always* get into fights."

Mallory took a deep breath. "I don't think you're stupid enough to have done it," she said, holding up a fist to show what she was going to do to whatever had. "But I don't think it was faeries, either."

Over dinner, their mother was oddly quiet as she slid chicken and mashed potatoes onto their plates. Mallory wasn't talking that much either, but Simon was going on and on about the tadpoles he had found and how they were going to be frogs in no time because they already had little arms.

Jared had seen them. They had a long way to go. What Simon called arms looked a lot more like fish zits.

"Mom?" Jared said finally. "Do we have a relative named Arthur?"

Their mother looked up suspiciously from her dinner. "No. I don't think so. Why do you ask?"

"I was just wondering," Jared mumbled. "What about Spiderwick?"

"That's your great-aunt Lucinda's surname," his mother said. "It was my mother's maiden name. Maybe Arthur was one of her relatives. Now, tell me why you want to know all this?"

"I just found some of his stuff in the attic—that's all," Jared said.

"In the attic!" His mother almost spilled her iced tea. "Jared Grace, as you know, half of the entire second floor is so rotted that if you step wrong, you'll find yourself in the downstairs parlor."

"I stayed on the safe side," Jared protested.

"We don't know if there is a safe side in the attic. I don't want anyone playing up there, especially you," she said, looking right at Jared.

He bit his lip. *Especially you.* Jared didn't say a thing for the rest of dinner.

"Are you going to read that all night?" Simon asked. He was sitting on his side of the room. Jeffrey and Lemondrop were running around on the comforter, and his new tadpoles were set up in one of the fish tanks.

"So what if I do?" Jared asked. With each crumbling page, Jared was learning strange facts. Could there really be brownies in his house? Pixies in his yard? Nixies in the stream out back? The book made them so real. He didn't want to talk to anyone right now, not even Simon. He just wanted to keep reading.

"I don't know," Simon said. "I thought maybe you'd be bored by now. You don't usually like to read."

Jared looked up and blinked. It was true. Simon was the reader. Jared mostly just got into trouble.

He turned a page. "I can read if I want to."

Simon yawned. "Are you worried about

falling asleep? I mean about what might happen tonight."

"Look at this." Jared flipped to a page close to the front. "There's this faerie called a brownie—"

"Like Girl Scouts?"

"I don't know," Jared said. "Like this. Look." He pushed the page in front of Simon. On the yellowed paper was an ink drawing of a little man, posed with a feather duster made from a badminton birdie and a straight pin. Next to it was a hunched figure, also small, but this one held a piece of broken glass.

"What's with that?" Simon pointed to the second figure, intrigued despite himself.

"This Arthur guy says it's a boggart. See, brownies are these helpful guys, but then if you make them mad, they go crazy. They start doing all these bad things and you can't stop

"Look at this."

them. Then they become boggarts. That's what I think we have."

"You think we made it mad by messing up its house?"

"Yeah, maybe. Or maybe it was kind of wacky before that. I mean, look at this guy"—Jared pointed to the brownie—"he's not the type to live in a skeevy house decorated with dead bugs."

Simon nodded, looking at the pictures. "Since you found the book in this house," he said, "do you think that this is a picture of *our* boggart?"

"I never thought of that," Jared said quietly. "It makes sense, though."

"Does it say in the book what we should do?"

Jared shook his head. "It talks about different ways to catch it. Not catch it for real, but see it . . . or get evidence."

"*Jared.*" Simon sounded doubtful. "Mom

Household Boggart

Small, vestigal wings

Wearing a child's shoes

Bugger stole my spectacles!

September 6th, 1909
The house was thought to be haunted;
however, it appears to be the handiwork
of a mischievous Boggart...

From the Field Guide

said to close the door and stay in here. The last thing she needs is another reason to believe that you were the one that attacked Mallory."

"But she thinks it was me anyway. If something happens tonight, she'll think it was me too."

"She won't. I'll tell her you were here all night. And besides, that way we can make sure nothing happens to either one of us."

"What about Mallory?" Jared asked.

Simon shrugged. "I saw her getting into bed with one of her fencing swords. I wouldn't mess with her."

"Yeah." Jared got into bed and opened the book again. "I'm just going to read a little more."

Simon nodded and got up to put the mice back in their tanks. Then he got into bed and pulled the covers over his head with a mumbled "good night."

As Jared read, each page took him deeper

nto the strange world of forest and stream, alive with creatures that seemed so close that he could almost stroke the slick, scaly flanks of the mermaids. He could almost feel the heat of the troll's breath and hear the rumble of the dwarven forges.

When he turned the last page, it was late at night. Simon was bundled up so that Jared could see only the top of his head. Jared listened hard, but the only sounds in the house were the wind whistling through the roof above them and water gurgling through the pipes. No scuttling or screaming. Even Simon's beasts were asleep.

Jared flipped to the page that read, *Boggarts delight in tormenting those they once protected and will cause milk to sour, doors to slam, dogs to go lame, and other malicious mischief.*

Simon believed him—sort of, anyway—but Mallory and their mom wouldn't. And besides, he and Simon were twins. It almost didn't count for anything that Simon believed him. Jared looked at the suggestion of the book: *Scattering sugar or flour on the floor is one way of obtaining footprints.*

If he had footprints to show, then they'd have to believe him.

Jared opened the door and crept downstairs. It was dark in the kitchen and everything was quiet. He tiptoed across the cool tile to where his mother had put the flour—in an old glass apothecary jar on the countertop. He took out several handfuls and scattered them liberally on the floor. It didn't look like much. He wasn't sure how well footprints would show up in it.

Maybe the boggart wouldn't even walk across the kitchen floor. So far, it seemed to stick to moving through the walls. He thought about what he knew about boggarts from the

Everything was quiet.

book. Malicious. Hateful. Hard to get rid of.

In their brownie form they were helpful and nice. They did all kinds of work for a plain old bowl of milk. Maybe . . . Jared went over to the fridge and poured milk into a small saucer. Maybe if he left it out, the creature would be tempted to come out of the walls and leave footprints in the flour.

But when he looked at the saucer of milk there on the floor, he couldn't help feeling a little bit bad and a little bit weird at the same time. In the first place, it was weird that he was down here, setting a trap for something that he didn't even know if he would have believed in two weeks ago.

But the reason he felt bad was . . . well, he knew what it was like to be mad, and he knew how easy it was to get into a fight, even if you were really mad at someone else. And he thought that just maybe that was how the boggart felt.

But then he noticed something else. He'd left footprints of his own in the flour all the way from the milk back to the hall.

"Crud," he muttered as he went to get the broom. The light cracked on.

"Jared Grace!" It was his mother's voice, coming from the top of the stairs.

Jared turned fast, but he knew how guilty he looked.

"Get back to bed," she said.

"I was just trying to catch—" But she didn't let him finish.

"Now, mister. Go."

After he thought about it for a minute, he was glad she'd interrupted him. His boggart idea probably wouldn't have been a big hit.

With a look back over his shoulder at the flour dusting the floor, Jared slunk up the stairs.

The kitchen was a mess.

Chapter Six

IN WHICH They Find
Unexpected Things in the Icebox

Jared rolled over at the sound of his mother's voice. She was angry. "Jared, you better get up."

"What's going on?" Jared asked sleepily, peering up from the covers. For a second he thought he'd missed school, until he remembered they'd moved and not even so much as set foot in the new school yet.

"Up, Jared!" his mother said. "You want to pretend you don't know? Fine, let's go downstairs so you can *see* what's going on."

The kitchen was a mess. Mallory had a

broom and was sweeping up broken pieces of a
porcelain bowl. The walls were painted with
chocolate syrup and orange juice. Raw eggs
oozed down the windowpanes.

Simon was sitting at the kitchen table. His
arms were covered with the same bruises
Mallory had been wearing only a day before, and
his eyes were red-rimmed, like he'd been crying.

"Well?" his mother asked expectantly.

"I—I didn't do this," Jared said, looking
around at them. They couldn't really believe he
would do something like this, could they?

And there, on the floor of the kitchen, next to
drifts of cereal and scattered pieces of orange
peel, Jared saw small tracks in the flour. They
were the size of his little finger, and he could
clearly see the imprint of the heel of a foot and a
feathering in the front that might have been
from toes.

"Look," Jared said, pointing. "See.
Little footprints."

Mallory looked up at him, and her
eyes were narrowed with fury.
"Just shut up, Jared. Mom says
she saw you down here last
night. You made those footprints!"

"I did not!" Jared yelled
back.

"Why don't you look in
the freezer then, huh?"

"What?" Jared asked.

Simon gave an especially
wet-sounding sob.

Their mother took the broom
from Mallory's hand and started sweeping up
the flour and cereal.

"Mom, no, the footprints," Jared said, but

his mother didn't pay any attention to him Two strokes of the broom, and the only proo he had was swept into a pile of rubbish.

Mallory opened the freezer door. Each o Simon's tadpoles was frozen into a single cub in the tray. Next to them was a note written i ink on a piece of a cereal box:

Not very nice to ice the mice.

"And Jeffrey and Lemondrop are gone! said Simon.

"Now, why don't you tell us what you di with your brother's mice?" said his mother.

"Mom, I didn't do it. I really didn't."

Mallory gripped Jared by the shoulder. " don't know what you think you're doing, bu you're about to start regretting it."

"Mallory," their mother cautioned. His siste

"Mom, I didn't do it."

let go, but the look she gave him carried the promise of later violence.

"I don't think Jared did it," said Simon between sniffs. "I think it was the boggart."

Their mother said nothing. The look on her face said that manipulating Simon was the worst thing Jared had done. "Jared," she said, "start taking this trash out to the front. If you thought this was funny, let's see how funny you think it is when you spend the rest of today cleaning it up."

Jared hung his head. He had no way of making her believe him. Silently, he got dressed, then gathered up three black garbage bags and started dragging them toward the front of the house.

Outside, the weather was warm and the sky was blue. The air smelled of pine needles and freshly mown grass. But daylight didn't seem to be any comfort at all.

One of the bags snagged on a branch, and when Jared tugged, the plastic ripped. Groaning, he dropped the bags and surveyed the damage. The tear was large, and most of the garbage had spilled out. As he started to gather things up, he realized what he was holding. The contents of the creature's house!

He looked at the worn bits of cloth, the doll's head, and the pins with pearl tops. In the daylight there were other things he had not noticed before. There had been a robin's egg, but it was crushed. Tiny slips of newspaper were scattered throughout, each one with a different strange word on it. "Luminous," read one. "Soliloquy," read another.

Gathering up all the pieces of the nest, Jared put them carefully aside from the rest of the trash. Could he make a new house for the boggart? Would it matter? Could that stop it?

He thought about Simon crying and about the poor, stupid tadpoles frozen in ice cubes. He didn't want to help the boggart. He wanted to catch it and kick it and make it sorry it ever came out of the wall.

Dragging the rest of the bags to the front lawn, he looked at the pile of the boggart's things. Still not sure whether he was going to burn them or give them back or what, he carried them inside.

His mother was standing in the doorway waiting for him. "What's all that?" she asked.

"Nothing," Jared said.

For once, she didn't question him. At least not about the junk pile in his hands.

"Jared, I know you're upset about your father leaving. We're all upset."

Jared looked at his shoes in discomfort. Just because he was upset about his father

There were other strange things.

leaving did not mean he had trashed their new house, or pinched his brother black and blue, or tied his sister's hair to her headboard. "So?" he asked, thinking that her silence meant she was waiting for a response.

"So?" she repeated. "*So* you need to stop letting your anger control you, Jared Grace. Your sister works things out when she's fencing and your brother has his animals, but you . . ."

"I didn't do it," Jared said. "Why won't you believe me? Is it because of the fight at school?"

"I have to admit," his mother said, "I was shocked to learn that you broke a boy's nose. That is just the kind of thing I'm talking about. Simon doesn't get into fights. And neither did you before your father left."

He studied his shoes even more intently. "Can I go inside now?"

She nodded, but then she stopped him with one hand on his shoulder. "If anything else happens around here, I'm going to have to take you to see someone. Do you understand?"

Jared nodded, but he felt weird. He remembered what he had said about Aunt Lucy and the nuthouse and suddenly felt very, very sorry.

"Mallory, no!"

Chapter Seven

IN WHICH the Fate of the Mice Is Discovered

"I really need your help," said Jared. His brother and sister were lying on the rug in front of the television. Each one had a controller, and from where he was standing, he could see colors flit across their faces as the screen changed.

Mallory snorted but didn't reply. Jared took that as a positive response. At this point, anything that didn't involve fists was a positive response.

"I know you think I did it," Jared said,

opening the book to the page about boggarts. "But, honest, I didn't. You heard the thing in the walls. There was the writing on the desk and the footprints in the flour. And remember

the nest? Remember how you guys pulled everything out of that nest?"

Mallory stood up and snatched the book out of his hands.

"Give it back," Jared pleaded, making a grab for it.

Mallory held it over her head. "This book is what started all the trouble."

"No!" Jared said. "That's not true. I got the book *after* your hair was knotted. Give it back, Mallory. Please give it back."

Now she held it in two hands, one on either side of the open book, poised to rip it apart.

"Mallory, no! No!" Jared was nearly speechless with panic. If he didn't think of something quick, the book was going to be in pieces.

"Wait, Mal," Simon said, getting up from the floor.

Mallory waited.

"What help did you want, Jared?"

Jared took a deep breath. "I've been thinking that if our messing up the nest is what got it upset, then maybe we could make it a new nest. I—I took a birdhouse and put some stuff in it.

"I thought—well—I thought that maybe the boggart was a little bit like us, because it's stuck here too. I mean, maybe it doesn't even want to be here. Maybe being here makes it mad."

"Okay, before I say I believe you," Mallory said, holding the book in a less threatening position, "tell me *exactly* what you want us to do."

"I need you guys to work the dumbwaiter," Jared said, "so I can bring the house up to the library. I thought it would be safe there."

"Let's see this house," Mallory said. She and Simon followed Jared into the hall, and he showed it to them.

It was made from a wooden birdhouse large enough for a crow to roost in. Jared had found it among the ones hung in the attic. Sliding up the back, he showed them how he had arranged everything except the cockroaches neatly inside. On the walls, he had taped up the newspaper words and also a few small pictures from magazines.

"Did you cut up Mom's stuff to make that?" Simon asked.

"Yeah," Jared said, and shrugged.

"You really did a lot of work," Mallory said.

"So you'll help me?" Jared

wanted to ask for the book back, but he didn't want to make his sister mad all over again.

Mallory looked at Simon and nodded.

"I want to go first, though," said Simon.

Jared hesitated. "Sure," he said.

Walking quietly past the den where their mother was phoning construction people, they went into the kitchen.

Simon hesitated in front of the dumbwaiter. "Do you think my mice are alive?"

Jared didn't know what to say. He thought about the tadpoles, frozen in ice. He wanted Simon to help but didn't want to lie.

Simon got down on his knees and climbed into the dumbwaiter. In a few moments, Mallory had wheeled him up inside the wall. Simon gave a small gasp as he started moving, but then they heard nothing, even after the dumbwaiter stopped.

"You said there was a desk in there and papers," Mallory said.

"Yeah." Jared wasn't sure what she was driving at. If she didn't believe him, she could ask Simon when he came back down.

"Well, they needed to get it in there somehow. And it wasn't little, right? So an adult worked in there—but how did an adult get in there?"

Jared was puzzled for a moment, then he understood. "A secret door?"

Mallory nodded. "Maybe."

The dumbwaiter came back down and Jared got inside, the little house cradled in his lap. Mallory winched him up inside the dark tunnel. The trip was fast, but he was still very, very glad to see the library.

Simon was standing in the middle of the room, looking around in awe.

Jared grinned. "See?"

"It's so cool in here," said Simon. "Look at all these animal books."

Thinking about the secret door, Jared tried to picture where he must be in relation to the rest of the rooms upstairs. He figured which direction would head toward the hall.

"Mallory thinks there's a hidden door," Jared said.

Simon came over. There was a bookcase, a large picture, and a cabinet in front of the wall Jared was looking at.

"Picture," Simon said, and together they took down the large oil painting. It was of a thin man with glasses sitting stiffly on a green chair. Jared wondered if that was Arthur Spiderwick.

Behind the picture was nothing but flat wall.

"Maybe we could pull out some of the

"It's so cool in here."

books?" Jared said, taking out one entitled *Mysterious Mushrooms, Fabulous Fungi.*

Simon opened the cabinet doors. "Hey, look at this." They opened into the upstairs linen closet.

A few minutes later, Mallory was looking around the room too.

"This place is creepy," Mallory said.

Simon grinned. "Yeah, and no one knows about it but us."

"And the boggart," said Jared.

He hung his birdhouse from a wall sconce. Mallory and Simon helped him make sure that the insides were arranged, and then each of them added something to the house. Jared put in one of his winter gloves, thinking that the boggart could use it as a sleeping bag. Simon added a small dish he'd once used to give his lizards water. And Mallory must have believed

Jared a little, because she tucked her silver fencing medal with the blue ribbon neatly inside.

When they were done, they looked it over. They all thought it was a fine house.

"Let's leave it a note," Simon suggested.

"A note?" Jared asked.

"Yeah." Simon pawed through the drawers of the desk and found some paper, a pen with a nib, and a bottle of ink.

"Hey, I didn't notice this," Jared said. He pointed to the watercolor painting of a man and a little girl on the desk. Underneath it in faint pencil was the inscription "my darling daughter Lucinda, age 4."

"So Arthur was her dad?" Mallory asked.

"I guess so," said Simon, clearing space on the desk to write.

"Let me do it," Mallory said. "You guys will take forever. Just tell what to write." She unstoppered the ink and dipped the pen. It made a scratchy but legible line on the paper.

"Dear Boggart," Simon started.

"Do you think that's polite?" Jared asked.

"I already wrote it," Mallory said.

"Dear Boggart," Simon said again. "We are writing you to say that we are sorry we messed up your first house. We hope you like what we

made and that even if you don't, that you'll stop pinching us—and other things—and that if you have Jeffrey and Lemondrop to please take care of them because they are good mice."

"Got it," Mallory said.

"Okay, then," said Jared.

They put the note on the floor near the little house and left the library.

Over the next week, none of them had time to visit the library, even through the linen closet. Construction people and movers were milling around the house during the day, and their mother was watching them closely at night, even going so far as to pace the hallways.

School had finally started, which wasn't as bad as Jared had feared. The new school was small, but it had a fencing team for Mallory, and no one was too mean to them their first couple of days there. So far, Jared had managed to behave.

Best of all, there were no more night attacks, no more scuttling in the walls — nothing other than Mallory's shorter hair to make it seem like the whole thing had really happened.

Except that Simon and Mallory were as eager to visit the room again as Jared was.

They got their chance one Sunday, when their mother went out shopping and left Mallory in charge. As soon as their mom's car pulled out of the driveway, they rushed up to the closet.

Inside the library, very little had changed. The painting leaned up against the wall, the birdhouse hung from the sconce, everything appeared to be just the way they'd left it.

"The note's gone!" announced Simon.

"Did you take it?" Mallory asked Jared.

"No!" Jared insisted.

There was the loud sound of a throat being cleared, and the three turned toward the desk. Standing on it, in worn overalls and a wide-brimmed hat, was a little man about the size of a pencil. His eyes were as black as beetles, his nose was large and red, and he looked very like the illustration from the Guide. He was holding a pair of leashes that attached to two gray mice that were sniffing the edge of the desk.

"Jeffrey! Lemondrop!" Jared squealed.

"Thimbletack likes his new house well," the little man said, "but that's not what he's come to tell."

Jared nodded, not sure what to say. Mallory looked like someone had smacked her in the face but she hadn't figured it out yet.

The mannikin went on. "Arthur Spiderwick's book is not for your kind. Too much about Fey for a mortal to find. All who have kept it have come to harm. Be it through violence or through charm. Throw the book away, toss it in a fire. If you do not heed, you will draw their ire."

"They? Who are they?" Jared asked, but the little man just tipped his cap and jumped off the side of the desk. He landed in the bright flood of sunlight in the open window and disappeared.

Mallory seemed to break out of her trance. "Can I see the book?" she asked.

Jared nodded. He'd taken to keeping it with him wherever he went.

Mallory knelt down and flipped through the pages with her fingers, quicker than Jared could read.

"Hey," Jared said. "What are you doing?"

About the size of a pencil

"Throw the book away."

Mallory's voice was weird. "I was just look-ing. I mean—this is a big book."

It wasn't a *small* book. "Yeah, I guess."

"And all these entries . . . all these *things* are real? Jared, that's a lot of real."

And then, suddenly, Jared understood what she was saying. If you looked at it that way, it was a big book, an absolutely huge book, too large to even comprehend. And worst of all, they were only at the beginning.

End of
BOOK ONE

About TONY DiTERLIZZI . . .

A *New York Times* best-selling author, Tony DiTerlizzi created the Zena Sutherland Award–winning *Ted, Jimmy Zangwow's Out-of-This-World Moon Pie Adventure*, as well as illustrations in Tony Johnston's Alien and Possum beginning-reader series. Most recently, his brilliantly cinematic version of Mary Howitt's classic *The Spider and the Fly* was awared a Caldecott Honor. In addition, Tony's art has graced the work of such well-known fantasy names as J.R.R. Tolkien, Anne McCaffrey, Peter S. Beagle, and Greg Bear as well as Wizards of the Coast's *Magic The Gathering*. He and his wife, Angela, reside with their pug, Goblin, in Amherst, Massachusetts. Visit Tony on the World Wide Web at www.diterlizzi.com.

and HOLLY BLACK

An avid collector of rare folklore volumes, Holly Black spent her early years in a decaying Victorian mansion where her mother fed her a steady diet of ghost stories and books about faeries. Accordingly, her first novel, *Tithe: A Modern Faerie Tale,* is a gothic and artful glimpse at the world of Faerie. Published in the fall of 2002, it received two starred reviews and a Best Book for Young Adults citation from the American Library Association. She lives in West Long Branch, New Jersey, with her husband, Theo, and a remarkable menagerie. Visit Holly on the World Wide Web at www.blackholly.com.

Tony and Holly continue to work day and night fending off angry faeries and goblins in order to bring the Grace children's story to you.

*You may know
the Grace kids well,
but there is still
much tale to tell. . . .*

*Like, who'd dare live
within a stream
beneath a bridge
where dark thoughts teem?*

TROLL

And where'd your
loose tooth really go?
To a friend?
Or to a foe?

HOGSQUEAL

Keep on reading,
and you will know.

THE SEEING STONE
BOOK TWO OF FIVE

ACKNOWLEDGMENTS

Tony and Holly would like to thank
Steve and Dianna for their insight,
Starr for her honesty,
Myles and Liza for sharing the journey,
Ellen and Julie for helping make this our reality,
Kevin for his tireless enthusiasm and faith in us,
and especially Angela and Theo—
there are not enough superlatives
to describe your patience
in enduring endless nights
of Spiderwick discussion.

The text type for this book is set in Cochin.
The display types are set in Nevins Hand and Rackham.
The illustrations are rendered in pen and ink.
Production editor: Dorothy Gribbin
Art director: Dan Potash
Production manager: Chava Wolin